VICKI C. HAYES

SADDLEBACK
EDUCATIONAL PUBLISHING

red rhino
b OO k s®

Blackout
Body Switch
The Brothers
The Cat Whisperer
Clan Castles
Clan Castles 2:
   Upgrade Pack
The Code
Fight School
Fish Boy
Flyer
The Forever Boy
The Garden Troll
Ghost Mountain

The Gift
The Hero of
   Crow's Crossing
Home Planet
I Am Underdog
Killer Flood
Little Miss Miss
The Lost House
The Love Mints
The Magic Stone
One Amazing
   Summer
Out of Gas
Please Don't Tell

Racer
Sky Watchers
The Soldier
Space Trip
Standing by Emma
Starstruck
Stolen Treasure
Stones
Too Many Dogs
World's Ugliest Dog
Zombies!
Zuze and the Star

SADDLEBACK
EDUCATIONAL PUBLISHING
www.sdlback.com

Copyright ©2016 by Saddleback Educational Publishing
All rights reserved. No part of this book may be reproduced in any form or by any means, electronic or mechanical, including photocopying, recording, scanning, or by any information storage and retrieval system, without the written permission of the publisher. SADDLEBACK EDUCATIONAL PUBLISHING and any associated logos are trademarks and/or registered trademarks of Saddleback Educational Publishing.

ISBN-13: 978-1-62250-978-2
ISBN-10: 1-62250-978-1
eBook: 978-1-63078-329-7

Printed in Malaysia

21 20 19 18 17   2 3 4 5 6

Jan

Age: 12

Biggest Secret: her real name is January

Favorite Vacation: the Girl Scouts father/daughter campout

Career Goal: to be a grief counselor

Best Quality: learns from her mistakes

CHARACTERS

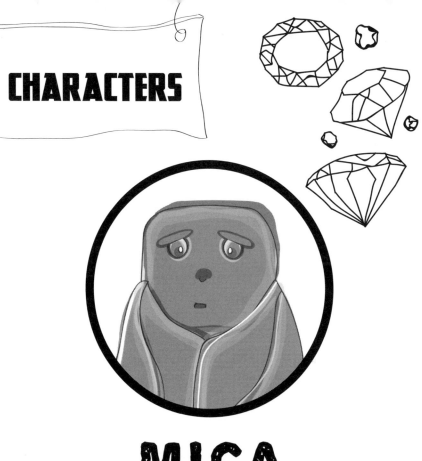

MICA

Age: 10

Hobby: gem hunting

Favorite Meal: fish and chips

Secret Wish: to visit New York City

Best Quality: never complains

1
NO FAIR

Jan was mad. She opened the back door. And walked into the kitchen. Her mom was there. She was cooking dinner. Jan dumped her backpack on the floor.

Her mom looked up at the loud thump. Emma was there too. She was stacking blocks.

"Hi, sweetie," her mom said. "You're just in time to set the table."

Jan pulled her long hair into a bun. "Do I have to?" she asked. "I'm tired."

"It would be helpful," said Mom.

Jan grabbed three plates and three glasses. She put them on the table. She scooped up some forks. She dropped them by the plates. Then she plopped down into a chair. She took out her phone.

How I set the table...

"How was school today?"

Jan read some texts on her phone. Her

mom stirred a pot on the stove. Jan didn't look up. She didn't talk. Mom got milk from the fridge. She looked at Jan.

"How's Abby?" her mom asked. "Did you make plans for the weekend?"

Jan tapped on her phone. She didn't look up. Her mom poured milk into two glasses. She glanced at Jan.

"How was the math test? Sixth grade can be pretty hard."

Jan banged her phone down on the table.

"It doesn't matter," she said loudly. "Nothing matters. Just leave me alone!"

"Jan," said Mom. "You don't need to be so angry. You're not the only one who misses Dad."

There was a crash. Emma's block tower had fallen. The blocks were everywhere. Jan kicked some blocks near her foot. Emma looked up at her sister. She looked sad.

"Pick them up," said Jan.

"Will you help me?" asked Emma.

Jan looked down at her little sister.

"Blocks are for babies," she said. "Play by yourself." Jan picked up her phone again.

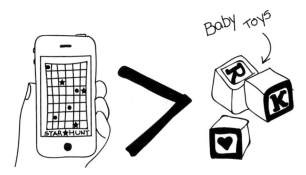

"Please?" asked Emma. She smiled at Jan. But Jan wasn't looking. Emma went back to her blocks.

"You could play with her a little," said Mom. "You don't play with her anymore."

Jan banged her phone down on the table again. She looked at her mom. "Stop telling me what to do!" she yelled. She stood up fast. Her chair fell over.

"Jan—"

"No! Everyone always tells me what to

5

do. My friends tell me. My teachers tell me. Emma tells me. You tell me," Jan said. "No one thinks of me. No one thinks of my feelings. They just boss me around. Dad *never* bossed me around."

Jan grabbed her phone. She got her backpack. The kitchen was too stuffy. She tore off down the hall. Why was everyone so awful?

She was angry. Her room was quiet. She went inside. Then slammed the door. Life wasn't fair! Why did her dad have to die?

Me and Dad. I really miss him.

Jan sat on her bed. She threw her stuffed bear against the wall. She fell back onto the soft covers. Turning over, she put her face into her pillow.

Nobody came to get her. Nobody said sorry.

Soon she was asleep.

2
JAN'S ROOM

Jan woke up. She was sweaty. Her back hurt. She rubbed her eyes. Why was it so dark in her room? What was wrong with her night-light?

Jan reached for her bedside lamp. She switched it on. Nothing happened. The lamp didn't work. *Must be a broken bulb,* she thought.

Why is this not working?!

9

Jan got up. She needed to change her damp clothes. There was a light switch by the door. She flipped the switch. It didn't move. Why was it stuck?

What's going on? she thought. The light was dim. But she saw shadows. Everything looked dark. And it also looked different. Weird-different. For one thing, there was no color.

Jan had a green quilt on her bed. The quilt looked gray now. She had many books on her desk. The books looked gray. Her window curtains had yellow flowers on them. The curtains looked gray too.

Where did the color go?

Was it the dark? Sometimes the dark made things look weird. Is that why everything looked gray?

That must be it, thought Jan. *I just need more light. Then everything will look okay.* Jan knew there was a streetlight outside her window. It was bright. She would use that light. Open the window. Feel the breeze. That was the plan.

She went to the window. And pushed back the curtains. She stared. The window was gone! Behind her curtains was a wall. A plain gray wall.

Maybe this was a dream. A scary dream.

Come on, Jan.
WAKE UP!

Jan ran to the bedroom door. She grabbed the handle and turned. The handle broke off in her hand. It wasn't made of metal. The handle felt light. Like paper.

"This is a crazy dream," said Jan. She pushed her messy hair off her face. "Mom!" she yelled. "Are you there?"

Jan banged on the door. But the door didn't feel like wood. It felt like paper too. Maybe she could tear it.

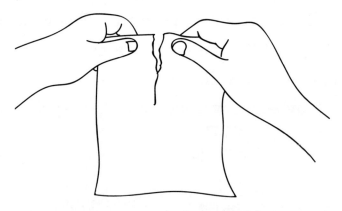

Jan moved away from the door. Then she ran. Fast. She ran right into the door. The door cracked. Jan pushed through it. She was out! She was out of her room!

But she wasn't in her house. She was in a cave.

3
THE CAVE

Jan stared. The cave was huge. The top was too high to see. There were big glowing rocks in the cave. The rocks made light. Jan looked back at her "bedroom." It looked like a large box. A large box sitting in a larger cave. What was going on?

Jan looked out into the cave again. She saw people. The people walked toward her. They took small careful steps. They looked strange.

My room?

Where am I?

I won't be scared of a dream, Jan thought to herself. She stared as the strange people came closer.

There were three of them. They were short. Their bodies were sort of square. Their skin was smooth and gray. Their heads were bald and gray. Their eyes were shiny and gray. Their robes were long and gray.

The shortest person shuffled up to Jan. "Welcome to Chertin," he said. "We are Cherts. I am Slate." He nodded his head to one side.

Jan took a step back. "Chertin?" she said. "Where's that?"

"Here," said Slate. "In Earth." He spread his arms wide.

Jan looked around the cave. She lifted her eyebrows. "What does that mean?" she asked. " 'In Earth'?"

"We are in Earth," said Slate. "We live here. In the caves."

Chertin

"We're under the ground?" asked Jan.

The Cherts nodded.

Jan glared at them. She put her hands on her hips. "Well, take me home," she said. "Have I been kidnapped? You can't do that!"

17

Slate looked down. He said nothing.

"Hey," said Jan. "Show me the path out. Now!" She stomped her foot.

Slate shook his head. "There is no path," he said. "You are three miles down. Three miles in the Earth."

Jan stared at Slate. "We're three miles below ground?" she asked. "How can you live here? How do you get light? How do you get air?"

Slate pointed at the glowing rocks. "Our light comes from glow stones," he said. "Our air comes from drill holes."

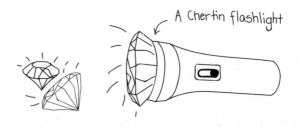

A Chertin flashlight

Jan glanced past Slate's pointing finger.

"Fine," she said. "So why am I here? Why is there a bedroom that looks like mine? But isn't."

"We want you to be happy," said Slate.

"Well, I'm not," said Jan. "The room was hot. The bed was hard. The lights didn't work. There was no window. And everything was gray."

It was like sleeping on a rock!

"We are sorry," said Slate. "We will try to fix it."

"Don't bother," said Jan. "I'm leaving as soon as I can."

"No," said Slate. "You cannot."

"What do you mean?" asked Jan. "Just take me back."

"No," said Slate again. "We need you here."

Jan opened her mouth. She was about to yell. But then something bumped into her legs. It knocked her to the ground. She landed hard on her back. Ouch! She closed her eyes.

4
MICA

Jan heard a cry. It sounded like Emma.

Oh, good, thought Jan. *My dream is over.* She opened her eyes. Wrong! She was still in the cave.

"We are sorry," said Slate. He was holding a young Chert. The young Chert was squirming to get down.

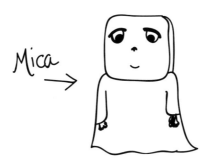

Mica →

"Who's that?" asked Jan. She sat up. Rubbed her back.

"This is Mica," said Slate.

Jan looked at Mica. He looked like the big Cherts. But he was her little sister's size. Maybe a bit bigger. Mica stared at Jan. He held out his hand.

Jan leaned back. "What does he want?" she asked.

"He wants you," said Slate. "Come with us. We'll show you why." He reached out to help Jan. But she stood up by herself.

"I'll come," she said. "But then I want to get out of here."

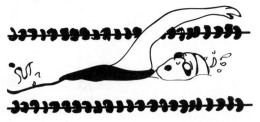

I can't miss swim practice tomorrow!

Slate put Mica down. The Cherts shuffled across the empty cave. Jan followed. They went into a smaller cave. This cave was full of Cherts. But these Cherts looked different. They were lying on stone beds. Their eyes were closed. Their skin was white. It was wrinkled. It was cracked.

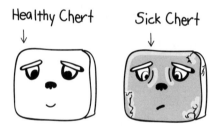

Healthy Chert ↓   Sick Chert ↓

"What's wrong with them?" asked Jan.

"They are sick," said Slate. "They are dying. We don't know why."

"Do you have doctors?" asked Jan.

Slate nodded. "Yes. But this sickness is new. We have no cure." He looked at Jan. "Not yet," he said.

23

Jan lifted her eyebrows.

"In Chertin, there is an old cave," said Slate. "This cave has wall paintings. Paintings from long ago. The paintings show Cherts with white skin. We didn't know why. Then some of us got sick. Some of us got white skin. Now we know what the paintings mean. They are showing a sickness from long ago."

"Okay," said Jan. "What's that got to do with me?"

"The paintings also show an upsider," said Slate.

"A what?" asked Jan.

"An upsider," said Slate. "Like you. In the paintings the upsider is near some Cherts. Those Cherts are standing. They look cured. The paintings tell us something. They tell us we need an upsider to cure us."

← An UPSIDER
UPSIDE down

Jan nodded. "Maybe," she said. "But why me?"

Slate shrugged. "You are the one who came," he said.

Jan frowned. "How can an upsider help?" she asked.

"We don't know," said Slate. "The paintings

don't tell us. Our doctors want to test you."

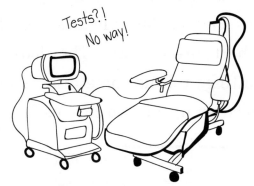

Tests?!
No way!

"I don't think so," said Jan. "No one is testing me. No way!" She turned to leave the cave.

Mica grabbed her hand. "Stay," he said.

Jan pulled her hand away. She turned to Slate. "Is he sick?" she asked.

"No," said Slate. "But his parents were. They both died. He wants you to help the others."

"He can't tell me what to do," said Jan. "He's just a kid." But she knew what it was like to lose a parent. Her dad was dead. She bent down to face Mica. "Look. I can't help you," she said. "I'm sorry."

Mica took Jan's hand again.

Jan looked up at Slate. "Get someone else," she said. "Not me. Send me home."

"We cannot," said Slate.

"Why not?" asked Jan. "How did you bring me here?"

"We found a machine," said Slate. "In the old cave. The machine was broken. Mica's parents worked hard to fix it. Then they got sick. They died before it was done. We kept working. Finally we fixed it. We turned it on. There was smoke. There were sparks. Then you came."

"So send me back," said Jan.

Slate pointed to a corner of the cave. Jan saw the machine. It looked burnt. Some parts had fallen off.

"It is broken again," said Slate. "We will try to fix it. But you will have to wait. Play with Mica. Be his friend."

Jan jerked her hand away from Mica. She glared at Slate. "Stop telling me what to do!" she yelled.

Jan ran from the small cave. She tore through the big cave. Where was her bedroom? There! She ran inside. Flopped onto the bed. And buried her face in the pillow.

I want to GO HOME!

5
PEBBLE

Jan heard footsteps. "Go away!" she yelled.

The footsteps stopped. Then Jan felt something. Someone was patting her hand. She turned her head to look. It was Mica. He stood next to the bed.

"Go away," said Jan again.

Mica reached out. He touched Jan's hair.

Jan pulled her head away. She sat up.

"Why are you here?" she asked. "I can't help you."

Mica got up onto the bed. He reached for Jan's hair again.

Jan looked at Mica. "Why don't you have hair?" asked Jan.

Mica shrugged.

"Never mind," said Jan. "Hair is a bother. Mom's always telling me to wash it. Brush it. Does your mom …" Jan stopped. She remembered that Mica's mom had died.

That's why I have so many hats!

Mica looked at her.

"I'm sorry," said Jan. "I'm sorry about your parents. My dad died last year. In a car crash. I was pretty sad."

Mica didn't say anything.

"I bet your life is hard," said Jan. "My life is hard. Everyone always yells at me. My friends. My teachers. My mom. My sister." She stopped talking.

Tuning everyone out...

Mica patted her hand again.

Jan frowned. "Go away," she said. "Go play with your friends. You must have friends."

Mica stayed on the bed.

"Go on." Jan gave him a push.

Mica slid off the bed. He left the room.

Good, thought Jan. She had a little sister. She did not need a little brother. Jan lay back down. She stared at the gray walls. Then she heard footsteps. Who was it now? She sat up.

It was Mica. He was back. Something was in his hand. He held it out.

Jan put out her hand. Mica dropped something into her palm. Something smooth. It was a stone. A glow stone. A little one. It sparkled. It looked like it had a light inside.

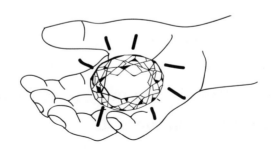

Jan stared at the stone. Then she smiled. She looked at Mica. "Thank you," she said.

Mica nodded. He reached for Jan's hand. He pulled her.

Jan stood up. "Are we going for a walk?" she asked.

Mica nodded. He led Jan out into the big cave.

For the next two days Mica stayed with Jan. He took her all over. He showed her caves of glow stones. Mica showed her drill holes. The holes blew cold air. The

Cherts breathed this air. Then he showed her a dark river. It was full of fish.

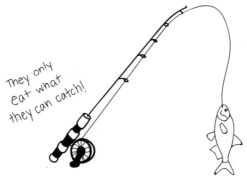

They only eat what they can catch!

Mica also showed her the cave of old paintings. They were faded and hard to see. In one painting Cherts were lying on the ground. They had white skin.

In another painting there was a man. He had clothes and hair. The man was human. An upsider.

In the last painting the Cherts were standing. The man was close to them. He was doing something. Jan couldn't see what it was. The painting was too old.

While Jan walked with Mica, she talked. She told Mica about her school. About her friends. About her real bedroom. About her family. And about her sister, Emma.

I miss my favorite reading chair!

And all my books!

Mica took Jan to a new cave. It was big. There were many Cherts. Some were sitting at tables, eating. Some were in beds, sleeping. Mica took Jan to one corner. Jan saw two little beds.

"What is this place?" she asked.

"Home," said Mica.

Jan was surprised. "There are two beds," she said. "Who sleeps in that one?"

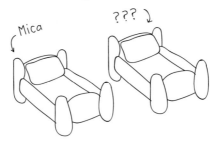

Mica pointed to a group of young Cherts. "Pebble," he said.

Jan saw a small Chert. Smaller than Mica. She was sitting on the ground. She was playing with glow stones.

"Your sister?" asked Jan.

Mica nodded.

Jan bent down. She smiled at Pebble. "Nice to meet you, Pebble," she said. Pebble did not look up. She played with her stones.

Mica took Jan's hand. He pulled her out of the cave.

Pebble

"Wait," said Jan. "I didn't know you had a sister. Shouldn't we talk to her? Play with her?"

Mica shook his head. He led Jan back to her room. He sat on her bed. But Jan wanted to talk.

"We need to help her," she said. "We need to take care of her. She's very little. She needs us. She needs *you*."

Mica didn't look at Jan. He lay on her bed.

"Mica," said Jan. "Get up. We need to help your sister." Jan went over to the bed. She looked at Mica.

37

Mica reached out his hand. Jan took it. Mica squeezed Jan's hand. She squeezed back.

"Mica?" she asked. "What's wrong?"

Mica looked strange. His skin was not gray. It was white. His skin was not smooth. It was wrinkled. Then Jan saw a crack. A crack on Mica's arm.

No! She gasped. Mica was sick.

6
SICK

"Mica!" yelled Jan. She ran out of her room. She ran into the big cave. "Help!" she called. "Mica's sick!"

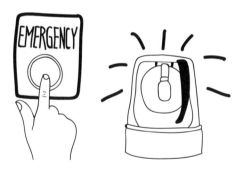

Some Cherts looked up. They came to Jan's room. They looked at Mica. The Cherts picked Mica up. They carried him out.

"Stop!" yelled Jan. "Where are you going?"

Slate came up to Jan. He looked sad. "He's going to the doctors," said Slate.

"Will he be all right?" asked Jan. "Can you help him?"

"No," said Slate. "He will die like all the rest." Slate turned to leave the room.

Jan grabbed his robe. "No," she said. "Let me help. I have to help. Take me to the doctors. They can test me. They can find out how I can help."

Slate nodded. He led Jan to the cave of sick Cherts. He led her to the doctors.

The doctors tested Jan's skin. They shook their heads. The doctors tested Jan's hair. They shook their heads again.

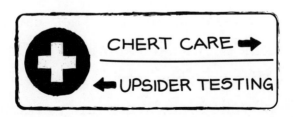

Jan went to look at Mica. His skin was very white. It was so wrinkled. His eyes were closed.

"Mica?" asked Jan. He reached out his hand. Jan took it. She squeezed Mica's hand. He squeezed back. A small squeeze. Jan looked at the doctors. "You must hurry," she said. "You must find a cure."

The doctors tested Jan's blood. They shook their heads a third time. Jan went to look at Mica again. His skin had many cracks. The cracks were everywhere. His eyes were closed.

What they gave me after taking my blood.

"Mica?" asked Jan. But he did not move. Jan picked up Mica's hand. It was cold. She squeezed his hand. Mica did not squeeze back.

"No!" yelled Jan. She dropped Mica's hand. She ran from the small cave. Her footsteps boomed in the big cave. She ran into her bedroom. She threw herself onto the bed. Her face was wet with tears. She cried and cried.

Mica was dead.

7
TEARS

Jan wiped her tears away. She was so tired. Then she heard soft footsteps. "Go away," she said.

I cried. A lot.

The footsteps stopped. Then Jan felt something. Someone was patting her hand. Jan turned her head to look. It was Pebble.

She was next to the bed. Jan stared at the little Chert.

Pebble touched Jan's hair. Jan picked her up. She put Pebble next to her. She hugged the little girl.

"I'm sorry," said Jan. "I'm sorry I couldn't help him."

I didn't know what to say...

Pebble didn't talk. She played with Jan's hair.

"Who will care for you now?" asked Jan. "You're all alone."

Pebble reached inside her robe. She pulled out some glow stones. She rubbed them. She gave one to Jan. Jan held it in her palm. The stone sparkled. It looked like it had a light inside.

"Thank you," said Jan. She gave Pebble another hug.

Jan carried Pebble to her cave. In Pebble's cave they played together. They played with glow stones. While they played, Jan talked about Mica.

"Your brother was sweet," said Jan. "He was caring. And kind."

Pebble and Jan put glow stones all over the cave. Then they sat on some chairs and looked around.

"This looks beautiful," said Jan. "We did a good job. Mica would have liked it."

Jan looked at Pebble. The little Chert

looked tired. She looked sad. She was very still.

"You remind me of Emma," said Jan. She picked Pebble up. "You need a nap," she said. She carried Pebble to her bed. And put her down. Pebble closed her eyes.

Pebble   Emma

Jan leaned over to give her a kiss. Then she saw something. Something on Pebble's cheek. It was a white spot. Jan's eyes opened wide. She took Pebble's arm. She pushed up her robe. There were more spots. White spots all over Pebble's arm.

Jan picked up the little Chert. She ran from the cave. Pebble had to see the doctors. Fast!

"Help!" cried Jan. "You must help. I can't lose Pebble too."

The doctors reached for Pebble. But Jan wouldn't let go. She hugged Pebble. She cried. Jan's tears dripped onto Pebble's robe. They dripped onto Pebble's face.

"Please be okay," she cried. "Please open your eyes."

Pebble opened her eyes. She looked at Jan's face.

Jan gave her a smile. "You'll be okay," she said. "I know you will."

Pebble blinked.

Jan wiped her tears off Pebble's cheek. Then she stopped. What was happening? "Look," said Jan to the doctors. "Look at the spots." She wiped Pebble's cheek again. The spots were fading. "This is it!" she said to the doctors. "This is what you need!"

The doctors took Jan's tears. They did some tests.

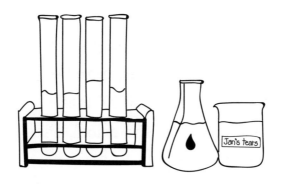

Jan stayed with Pebble. The little girl's skin was white. It was wrinkled. Her eyes were closed again.

The doctors came back. They did not shake their heads.

One doctor went to Pebble. She gave the little girl a shot. "We must wait," she said.

Jan nodded. But she was tired. She had cried so much. She needed to rest. The ground next to Pebble's bed was hard. But it would have to be okay. She lay down. Closed her eyes. And slept.

Jan felt someone patting her hand. She looked up. It was Pebble. She was leaning over from her bed. Her skin was gray. Normal!

Jan laughed. "They did it!" she cried. "They cured you." She gave Pebble a big hug. "You're getting better."

But Pebble did not look happy. She pointed to Jan's arm. Jan looked. Her own arm was very white. Her skin was wrinkled. Jan looked back at Pebble. Pebble's eyes were wide.

"Don't die," said Pebble.

8
GOODBYE

Jan pulled herself up. She went to the doctor. "Am I sick?" she asked. She held up her arm. "Am I going to die?"

What is happening to me?

The doctor looked at Jan. He checked her arm. He checked her face.

"You do not have the same sickness," he said. "You have something else. We call it cave sickness."

"What's that?" asked Jan.

"Cave sickness is from bad air," said the doctor. "The air in our caves is good for us. But it is bad for you. It is making you sick. You must leave. Or you will die."

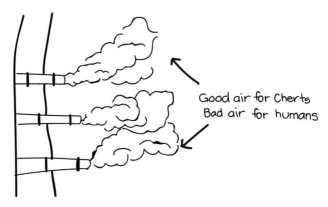

Good air for Cherts
Bad air for humans

"I can't leave," said Jan. She looked back at Pebble.

"You have to leave," said the doctor. "I will tell Slate."

Jan went back to Pebble's bed. "I want to stay," said Jan. She took Pebble's hand. "I want to help you."

Pebble pushed Jan's hand away. She shook her head. Pebble looked at the wall.

"Don't you want me to stay?" asked Jan. "We can go for walks. We can play with glow stones."

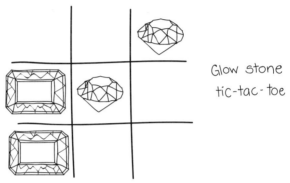

Glow stone
tic-tac-toe

Pebble shook her head.

Jan looked sad.

Then the doctor came back. Slate was with him. Slate walked up to Jan. "Follow me," he said. He went out into the big cave. Jan followed him. "We think the machine is ready," he said.

"But what about Pebble?" asked Jan.

"What will happen to her? Who will care for her?"

Maybe she could come with me?

"We will care for her," said Slate. "She is almost cured. Thanks to you."

Jan gave him a little smile.

"But you must leave," said Slate. "If you don't, you will die. We are ready to send you home."

Jan sighed. She had wanted to go home for a long time. But now she wanted to stay. She wanted to be with Pebble.

"Can I say goodbye?" she asked.

Slate nodded.

Jan walked back into the small cave.

Pebble was sitting up in bed. She was playing with a pile of glow stones. The little Chert looked up when Jan came in. Then she looked away.

Jan sat on Pebble's bed. She patted Pebble's hand. "I came to say goodbye," she said. "I'm going home."

Pebble turned to face Jan. She had tears in her eyes. Jan held out her arms. Pebble fell into Jan's arms. They hugged for a long time.

Finally Jan stood up. She touched Pebble's cheek. Pebble picked up two glow stones. She put them into Jan's hand.

Pebble pointed to each stone. "Mica," said the little girl. "Pebble."

Jan closed her hand around the stones. "I will remember," said Jan. Then she turned and left the cave.

9
JAN'S ROOM

Jan woke up. It was dark. Was she home? Was she in her real bedroom?

She hopped off the bed. She went to the light switch. Flipped it. The lights came on.

Jan looked at her bed. Her quilt was green. She looked at the curtains. There were yellow flowers on them. She went to the window. Pushed back the curtains. There was the window. The sun was just coming up. She was home!

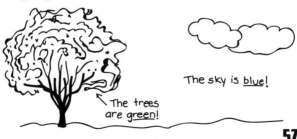

The sky is <u>blue</u>!

The trees are <u>green</u>!

Jan opened the door to her room. She ran down the hall. She ran into the kitchen. Mom was at the stove. She was making eggs. Emma was in her chair. She was eating cereal.

"I'm back!" said Jan. She grinned at Mom. She grinned at Emma.

Mom looked up. She frowned. "Good," she said. "Have a seat. Breakfast is ready."

My favorite!

Emma kept eating.

Jan stood by the door. She stared at her family. "Weren't you worried?" she asked.

"Honey, I'm sorry," said Mom. "I didn't

mean to get angry last night. I was tired.
Let's try to be better with each other." She
put some eggs on Jan's plate.

"Last night?" said Jan. "That wasn't last
night. I've been gone! For three days!"

Mom looked up. "Please, Jan," she said,
frowning. "No more games. It's Saturday
morning. Just eat your breakfast."

It was
real!

THEY were
real!

Jan walked slowly to the table. "Mom,
listen," she said. She sat down. "I've been
gone for three days. I went inside the Earth.
I visited these people called Cherts. They
were sick. They were dying. They needed a

human. And they got me. Mica died. But Pebble didn't. She got better. I helped them. It was my tears."

← The cure

Mom looked sad. She sat beside Jan. "I know it's been hard," she said. She patted Jan's hand. "Without Dad. I'm glad you had a happy dream."

Jan pulled her hand away. "It wasn't a dream!" she yelled. "It was real. I *did* help them." Jan pushed her plate away. She stood up.

Emma began to cry.

"Stop crying," yelled Jan. "Pebble never cried. You're just a baby."

"Don't yell at her," said Mom. "She *is* a baby. Sit down and eat."

"No," said Jan. "You don't understand me. The Cherts did. They *needed* me. I want to go back. I hate this family!"

Jan rushed from the kitchen. She ran to her room. And slammed the door. She flung herself down onto the bed.

Why was everything still awful? Why was her family still the same?

10
NEEDED

Jan lay on her bed. She thought about Mica. Was Mom right? She thought about Pebble. Had it been a dream?

Some of the dream was sad. Mica had died. But some was good. Jan had saved Pebble and the others. That made her feel happy.

Why didn't she feel happy back at home? Why did she feel mad again?

Finally home →
but I miss Chertin...

Jan thought about Mica. His life had been sad. But he hadn't been mad. He had been kind. Helpful. He had cheered Jan up.

Jan thought about Pebble. Her life had been sadder. But she hadn't been mad. She had been sweet. And she had cared for Jan. She wanted Jan to live. She told Jan to leave Chert. Even if it meant she would be alone.

But Jan wasn't alone. She had a family. She didn't need to be sad.

Jan thought about her mom. Mom never smiled anymore. She worked hard at her job. She cared for Jan and Emma. But she wasn't happy. She missed Dad.

Mom never plays the piano anymore. She used to love it.

Jan thought about Emma. Emma never laughed anymore. No one played with her. No one tickled her. No one told her silly jokes. She wasn't happy. She missed Dad.

Emma missed riding around on Dad's shoulders.

Mom and Emma needed someone. Someone to help them feel happy.

"They need me," said Jan. "I can be like Mica and Pebble." She went back down the hall.

Outside the kitchen door she heard a voice. It was Emma.

"Mommy, play with me," said Emma. "Please …"

She's whining again, thought Jan. *I can't do this. I can't help them.*

She turned around. Shoved her hands into her pockets. She felt two things, small and round. She knew what they were. Slowly she turned back toward the kitchen.

Jan heard Emma again. "I need someone," said Emma. "Someone to play with me."

Emma's voice sounded different. She didn't sound whiny. She sounded lonely.

"I don't have time, honey," said Mom. "I've got too much to do."

← Just 3 days worth ... poor Mom.

Mom's voice sounded different too. She didn't sound mad. She sounded sad.

Jan took a deep breath. *Mica and Pebble helped me,* she thought. *I can help my family.*

Jan walked into the kitchen. She went over to her mom. "I'm sorry, Mom," she said. She gave her mom a hug. "I didn't mean to get mad. Thanks for making breakfast."

Jan's mom smiled.

Jan sat at the table beside Emma. The little girl sniffed.

"Hey, Emma," said Jan. "I was thinking. Maybe we could go to the park."

Emma loves feeding the ducks

Emma looked up at her big sister. Her eyes opened wide. She nodded.

"And look. I have something I want to show you." Jan reached into her pocket. She pulled out the small stones. Then put them on the table in front of Emma.

The stones sparkled. It was like there was a light inside them.